Perfectly POPPY

Party Pooper

Story by Michele Jakubowski

Pictures by Erica-Jane Waters

Picture Window Books

Perfectly Poppy is published by Picture Window Books, a Capstone Imprint
1710 Roe Crest Drive, North Mankato, Minnesota 56003
www.capstonepub.com

Library of Congress Cataloging-in-Publication Data
Jakubowski, Michele, author.
Perfectly Poppy party pooper / by Michele Jakubowski ; illustrated by Erica Jane Waters.
pages cm -- (Perfectly Poppy)
Summary: At the big neighborhood summer party Poppy eats too many treats, and gets an upset stomach.
But she does not want to be left out when the other children are having so much fun.
ISBN 978-1-4795-2282-8 (hardcover) -- ISBN 978-1-4795-2356-6 (pbk.)
1. Block parties--Juvenile fiction. 2. Group games--Juvenile fiction. [1. Parties--Fiction.
2. Games--Fiction.] I. Waters, Erica-Jane, illustrator. II. Title. III. Title: Party pooper.
PZ7.J153555Pg 2014
813.6--dc23   2013027849

Designers: Heather Kindseth Wutschke and Kristi Carlson

Printed in the United States of America in North Mankato, Minnesota.
092013   007766CGS14

Table of Contents

Chapter 1
Party Prep

"I can't wait for the party tonight!" Poppy said to her best friend, Millie.

"Me too," Millie agreed.

Every summer, the families in Poppy and Millie's neighborhood had a big outdoor party.

"I wonder what games we'll play

this year," Millie said.

Her favorite part of the party was

playing games.

"I wonder what kind of food there will be," Poppy said.

Her favorite part of the party was the food. In fact, her favorite part of every party was the food.

"We're going to bring s'mores," Millie said with a big smile.

"Snores?" Poppy asked.

"No, silly! S'mores," Millie said, laughing. "First you roast a marshmallow on the fire. Then you put it between graham crackers and a piece of chocolate."

Poppy loved anything with

chocolate!

"They are so good you want to

eat some more. Get it?" Millie asked.

"S'more?"

"Oh, I get it," Poppy said. "And I

can't wait to try one!"

Chapter 2

Home Free

The party started at four o'clock

and was in full swing by five. The

yard looked great, and the weather

was perfect. Everyone was having

lots of fun.

Poppy's mom was busy, so Poppy
decided to eat whatever she wanted.
Her mom didn't even notice! She ate
chips, candy, and more chips.

"Do you want some grapes?"

Millie asked.

"No thanks. I really like these

chips," Poppy said.

"What about the s'mores later?"

Millie asked.

"I can eat those, too," Poppy said.

"Okay. But my dad says if you eat too much junk food you'll feel sick," Millie said.

"I'll be fine. Anyway, I'm stuffed," Poppy said. "Let's go watch some TV."

"No way!" Millie said. "The games
are starting!"

"I'm pretty tired," Poppy said.

"It's probably from eating so much
junk food," Millie said.

"No, it's not," Poppy said.

Just then, her older brother Nolan came over.

"We're playing tag, and you're 'it'!" he yelled as he ran away.

Even though she was tired, Poppy jumped up. She didn't want to seem like a party pooper.

Poppy chased a lot of people and was glad when she finally tagged Emma.

After tag, everyone jumped rope.

Then they had bike races.

"Let's play Home Free! I'll be 'it,'"
Nolan said.

Then he explained the rules.

A bucket was home base. The person who was "it" guarded the bucket. Everyone had to hide. Then kids would run to kick the bucket yelling "Home Free!" as the person who was "it" tried to tag them.

Poppy frowned. She was really tired now, and her stomach hurt.

"What's wrong?" Millie asked.

"Nothing," Poppy lied. She didn't want Millie to know that she was right about eating all that junk food.

"Cheer up! After this game we will finally get our s'mores," Millie said.

Poppy tried to look excited, but it was hard.

"Hooray," she said quietly as she went to hide.

Chapter 3
S'more Time

As Poppy sat behind a big tree, she decided to rest. She felt very smart. Nobody would even notice she wasn't playing the game.

Poppy heard Millie and James yell "Home Free!" They both got past Nolan.

Poppy saw Jason on the other side
of the yard. He looked like he was
going to run for the bucket. Poppy
knew that if Nolan went after Jason,
she could kick the bucket safely.

Sitting alone was boring. Her stomach still hurt, but she knew what she had to do. Maybe getting up and moving would help her feel better.

"Home Free!" she yelled.

Poppy ran for the bucket as fast as she could. Nolan wasn't fast enough to catch Jason and Poppy.

"Nice job!" Millie said.

"Thanks," Poppy said. She was still tired, but sometimes tired felt good.

Poppy's mom called the kids over for s'mores.

"Finally!" Millie said. "I bet you
are super excited."

"Ummm . . . not really. I'm not
very hungry," Poppy said.

"You never say that!" Millie said.

"I think I ate too much junk food," Poppy said.

"You really aren't going to have a s'more?" Millie asked.

"Nope. But I will be ready to have s'more fun once you are done eating," Millie said.

"Very funny," said Millie as she happily ate her treat.

"Funny and full," Poppy said with a smile. "What a day!"

Poppy's New Words

I learned so many new words today! I made sure to write them down so I could use them again.

agreed (uh-GREED) — shared the same opinion or said yes

boring (BOR-ing) — not interesting

explained (ek-SPLAYND) — made something easier to understand

guarded (GARD-id) — protected or watched

neighborhood (NAY-bur-hud) —local area around your house

stuffed (STUHFT) — filled with too much food

Poppy's Ponders

After the big party I had some time to think. Here are some of my questions and thoughts from the day.

1. Did you know why I wasn't feeling good? Were there any clues in the story or art to support your answer?

2. When you go to a party, what is your favorite part? The food, games, or something else? Talk about your answer.

3. I learned a good lesson about not eating too much junk food. Write about a time that you learned a good lesson.

4. Write a newspaper article about our neighborhood party.

Kick the Can

We played a game called Home Free. It's kind of like the game Kick the Can, which is also a lot of fun. Here are the rules:

1. Pick someone to be "it."

2. Place the can in the center of your playing area (it can be a soda can, a bucket, or anything else that you can kick).

3. The person who is "it" closes his/her eyes and counts to twenty-five. During this time, everyone else runs and hides.

4. When the person who is "it" sees someone hiding, they call out his/her name.

5. The hider and the "it" person race back to the can.

6. If the "it" person kicks the can first, the hider is put in jail. If the hider kicks the can first, anyone in jail is free and can hide again.

7. The "it" person either counts again or keeps looking for more hiders, depending on who gets to the can first.

8. The game continues until everyone is found. The last person found is "it" for the next game.

About the Author

Raised in the Chicago suburb of Hoffman Estates, Michele Jakubowski has the teachers in her life to thank for her love of reading and writing. While writing has always been a passion for Michele, she believes it is the books she has read throughout the years, and the teachers who assigned them, that have made her the storyteller she is today. Michele lives in Powell, Ohio, with her husband, John, and their children, Jack and Mia.

About the Illustrator

Erica-Jane Waters grew up in the beautiful Northern Irish countryside, where her imagination was ignited by the local folklore and fairy tales. She now lives in Oxfordshire, England, with her young family. Erica writes and illustrates children's books and creates art for magazines, greeting cards, and various other projects.